Bridget Jones's
Guide to Life

Bridget Jones's Guide to Life

Helen Fielding

PICADOR

First published 2001 by Picador
an imprint of Macmillan Publishers Ltd
25 Eccleston Place, London SW1W 9NF
Basingstoke and Oxford
Associated companies throughout the world
www.macmillan.com

ISBN 0 330 48857 0

Comic Relief and Macmillan Publishers Ltd would like to thank
Delia Smith and BBC Worldwide for allowing Bridget Jones to pinch and adapt
her recipe for 'Terrine of Venison with Juniper and Pistachio Nuts'.

Lyrics from 'I will survive' (Perren/Fekaris) by kind permission
of Universal Music Publishers Ltd.

3 5 7 9 8 6 4 2

A CIP catalogue record for this book is available
from the British Library.

Typeset by Macmillan General Books Department
Printed and bound in Great Britain by
Mackays of Chatham plc, Chatham, Kent

Preface

There are times in one's life – for example when one says such things as 'Oh God, I'm starving', then eats a chocolate croissant then has a panic attack as there are 400 calories in it and spends the rest of the day getting weighed – when one suddenly thinks 'Oh'. For what would people who are really starving in Africa think about one?

It is very complicated, as many matters such as world politics and the debt crisis are to blame (see experts, *The Economist*, etc.) But the point is if in one half of the world people are trying to stop themselves eating food in case they can't fit into their skirts, and in the other half of the world people are trying frantically to find something to eat because if they don't they will die, then it is perfectly obvious that it is not so much complicated as not fair.

This is why it is good to take an interest in world politics and also to buy this book, even if some bits of it are not that good (see Accounting p.21) as two pounds goes to Comic Relief. Also Comic Relief are not just rushing out sacks of grain in a crisis with all celebrities dripping over babies, but trying to set up more substantial items such as farming methods, wells, health schemes, etc. so it makes things slightly more secure for people who are living on such a knife edge of existence that the smallest crisis pushes them completely over the edge. So it is definitely good, I think. And then I think it is OK for the time being about getting weighed all the time. Even though it is a bit stupid really. But then so are a lot of things.

B. Jones

Contents

The Fragrant Home

It is never good to have things
rotting around the place.

Household Management

A warm fire flickering in the grate, fresh flowers, sparkling crockery and glassware, the comforting aroma of baking bread, freshly ground coffee and the scent of lilies – the welcoming home!!

Not that good housekeeping is about pleasing men, as that would be subjugating oneself to the paternalistic sexist bastards and giving way to centuries of oppression; but just say you have got someone coming round who you might want to shag, it is always nice to have the flat looking good and smelling fragrant to create a pleasing sense that it is like that all the time.

Flowers

These are readily available at petrol stations. Simply take the polythene and string or rubber bands off and put them in a vase or something, then put water in.

(Remember to chuck them away after a couple of weeks or the water really stinks.)

Fire

The key words here are 'in the grate'. Fires in the kitchen or other household areas play no part in the desired overall effect and may make people think you are a bit all over the place. So if you have a gas hob, remember to keep flammable items such as tea towels and magazines well away from the burner, and don't try to light candles by setting fire to a rolled-up piece of newspaper and using it as a taper. Better to actually bring the candles to the hob (if time).

(N.B. *Fire safety*: When lighting cigarettes from the hob, always hold them in your hand and not your mouth as this can singe your eyelashes.)

Sparkling crockery and glassware

Before receiving guests, find glasses and mugs in all areas of flat and put in the dishwasher. (Remember to turn it on.)

Fragrance

1 Get loaf of bread.

2 Put in oven and turn on.

3 Oh yes. Remove polythene bag if bread is in it.

The delicious aroma of baking bread will thus fill your flat! (Remember to turn the oven off after a bit or bread will set on fire – see 'Fire' above.)

To Create a Pleasingly Ordered Bedroom

Expecting attractive bedroom visitor? Plagued by things all over floor? Simply follow easy step-by-step guide to transform your most intimate space into impressively ordered enclave.

1 Push all things under bed.

2 Some persistent items may still protrude tellingly from under bed.

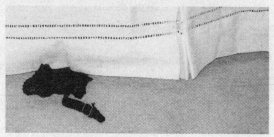

3 Push persistent items further under bed.

4 There.

Cookery
(or Cuisine)

What distinguishes haute cuisine from everyday
food is *concentration* of taste.

The Art of Cuisine

I am not a chef. I am not even a trained or professional cook. However, I do have strong things to say about cooking and important principles, such as escape from the tyranny of the recipe.

One must always have basic rules at the heart of one's approach to anything. Here – before I share my favourite dishes – are mine in the world of cuisine.

1 It is best if possible not to try actually to cook anything.

2 It is impossible to overestimate the importance of timing – a good cook is a strategist as well as a craftsman – always have everything you will need ready before you start, e.g. phone numbers, cash, names of restaurants, take-aways, etc.

3 Do not become enslaved to the tyranny of the recipe.

Cheese

1 Find bit of cheese in fridge.

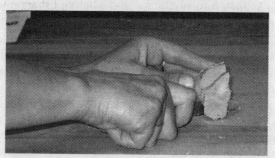

2 Cut off mould.

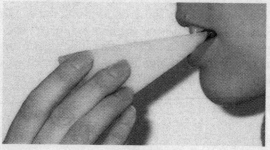

3 Eat.

The Adaptable Cook

'Adapt and survive'
C. Darwin (or A. Einstein?)

As every woman knows, there are times in one's life when one's principles are violated. There may be occasions – such as when one has been invited to about forty-three psychologically tortureful Smug Married dinner parties ('How's your love life? More wood-oven corn-fed burrito?' etc. etc.) and feels one simply must return hospitality to others.

At such times it may be necessary actually to cook, and on such occasions recipes can be good as long as one does not feel one has to stick to every single itsy-bitsy detail about this ingredient or that ingredient or fine grate zest this or marinate for two hours that.

To that end here is a favourite example of how to adapt a recipe to the busy demands of the working woman's life. In town most game is a luxury and in winter the best restaurants feature it on their menus. It is usually served carefully carved or boned on its dainty bed of vegetables.

Terrine of Venison with Juniper and Pistachio Nuts

SERVES 10-12

This is just about the easiest terrine in the world to make because you can buy the venison and the pork ready minced. The result is a lovely, rough country pâté. Serve it with thick slices of toasted country bread, and an excellent accompaniment would be the Confit of Cranberries on page 43.

1 lb (450 g) minced venison, available in large supermarkets	1 heaped teaspoon chopped fresh thyme
1 lb (450 g) ready-minced pork	2 rounded teaspoons salt
8 oz (225 g) rindless smoked streaky bacon	6 oz (175 ml) dry white wine
30 juniper berries, crushed	1 fl oz (25 ml) brandy
1 rounded dessertspoon mixed peppercorns	
4 oz (110 g) ready-shelled pistachio nuts	
¼ teaspoon powdered mace	

You will also need a 2-lb (900-g) loaf tin 7½ x 4¾ x 3½ inches (19 x 12 x 9 cm) deep, preferably non stick, or a terrine of 3-pint (1.75-litre) capacity.

Pre-heat the oven to gas mark 2, 300°F (150°C).

First of all, place the venison and the pork in a large bowl then place the bacon slices on a board stacked on top of one another and cut them into thin strips about ⅛ inch (3 mm), then add these to the bowl. After that crush the juniper berries quite coarsely with a pestle and mortar, add these to the bowl then crush the peppercorns, also quite coarsely, and add these. To deal with the pistachio nuts all you need to do is chop them in half, then they can go in along with the thyme, mace, salt and then finally the wine and brandy.

Now you've got quite a lot of mixing to do, so either use your hands or take a large fork and thoroughly combine everything. Cover the bowl with a cloth and leave it all to marinate for about 2 hours, then pack it into the loaf tin or terrine and cover the surface with a double thickness of foil, pleat the corners and fold it under the rim. Now place the terrine in a roasting tin and put it on the middle shelf of the oven, then pour in about 1 inch (2.5 cm) of boiling water from the kettle and let the terrine cook for 1¾ hours. After that, remove it from the oven, leaving the foil on, then after 30 minutes place two 1 lb (450 g) weights on top or the equivalent in tins of tomatoes or something similar. When the terrine is completely cold, place it in the fridge with the weights still on top and leave it overnight to really firm up. Don't forget to take it out of the fridge about an hour before serving, and serve cut in slices.

◇

Pizza

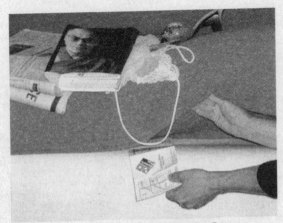

1 Find Domino's Pizza leaflet
thing with pizzas on.

2 Choose pizza.

3 Ring up Domino's Pizza and order pizza.

4 Wait for pizza.

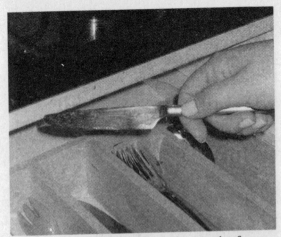

5 Maybe, if time allows, get out knife.

6 When door bell rings, pay pizza man and receive pizza into home.

7 Open box.

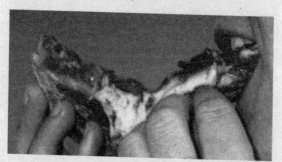

8 Eat pizza.

9 Have cigarette to get through remorse
re: calories contained in pizza.

The store cupboard

A well-stocked store cupboard is the key to not having to go out to the shops too much. Here are my top five store cupboard must-haves:

- Silk Cut
- 4 bottles of white wine
  (at least – you never know who will come round)
- Matches
- Canapés (i.e. crisps)
- Not marmite*

   * As may make one depressed if no bread.

The fridge too is important. These are all excellent fridge staples:

- Milk

Milk is of course ideal but a delicate product which requires constant attention. Always smell before serving.

- Cheese

Cheese is good because even if it starts to go off you can usually find a bit in the middle which is OK. See p.9.

– Eggs

Many people believe that eggs don't go off, but they do, so watch it.

– Vegetables

Vegetables keep well in the fridge. But lettuce isn't great because it rots after a while even if you buy it washed in a bag. Also remember that woman in the papers who opened the bag and there was a live toad** in it. (Actually, come to think of it, I'm not sure I really like vegetables. If they weren't non-fattening I definitely wouldn't eat them.)

– Chocolate

Chocolate is the foodstuff most suited to fridge storage. It is always delicious when chilled.

Fridge magnets are nice.

** The above reminds me of when we were at school and used to work at the pork pie factory in the holidays and have a competition as to who could put the worst thing in a pork pie. The worst I put in was a washing-up cloth but some girls were really quite outrageous. The most worrying thing was that no one ever reported finding anything amiss with their pies. But then that's pork pies for you, isn't it?

Advanced Cuisine

For:

- Making pickles, chutneys and preserves
- Wild boar and its accompaniments
- Chucking oysters
- Curing and salting meats
- Zesting citrus fruits
- Boning a hare
- Gluten
- Filleting and skinning flat fish
- Thickening agents
- Furred game

see p.20, 'Advanced Menu'.

Late night impromptu snack

This is delightful for impromptu late night after-theatre-type snacks (is not necessary to actually go to the theatre, obviously as v. embarrassing occasion with real actors only a few feet away talking in actory voices).

1 Get pitta bread.

2 Get other things which may be in fridge, e.g. cheese.

3 Put inside pitta bread. (Have to cut it first but is hollow in middle so can get things in.)

4 Put in microwave (remove non microwavable items from inside pitta bread first e.g. lettuce, tinfoil).

5 Wait calmly till finished. Not to be like Elizabeth Taylor standing in front of microwave shouting: 'Hurry!' Take out (but see below).

6 If goes all hard do another one if bread available only don't put it in for so long. Do not put your hand in when microwave is going because once a chef did this over and over again and it cooked his arm. Like meat.

7 Cut up and serve in attractive wedges.

8 Add garnish (leaf of some kind?) (A good cook is an artist as well as a craftsman.)

9 Eat (but not garnish if garnish is leaf from street outside).

Advanced Menu

I haven't got onto this yet, sorry and everything.

Accounting

'A woman should be a whore in
the bedroom, a cook in the kitchen and an
accountant in the accounting room.'

(J. Hall?)

Accounting

This is a bad thing.
(Apparently, the idea is to write everything down in lines.)

Social and Sexual Etiquette

Good manners means the ability to make
other people feel comfortable (unless they are rude
Smug Marrieds, then it means the ability
to make other people shut up).

The Art of Conversation

The art of conversation is a delicate thing. The main thing is not to put your foot in it. Here are some illustrations from the world of Sexual Relations, Smug Married-dom and Finance.

Bad things for men to say during sex

- 'Damn, I must take the car into the Citroen garage.'
- 'Oooh, you're all squashy.'
- 'This is just a bit of fun, right?'
- 'Britney, Britney . . .'

Bad things for you to say during sex

- 'Do you love me?'
- 'Is it in yet?'
- 'Leave no seed.'
- 'Fill me with your babies.'

Bad things for men to say on seeing you first thing in the morning

– 'Gaaah!'

– '. . . And you are?'

Good things to say to Smug Marrieds when they ask you why you're not married yet

– 'I'm not married because I'm a Singleton, you smug, prematurely ageing, narrow-minded morons. And because there's more than one way to live: a quarter of all households are single, the nation's young men have been proved by surveys to be completely un-marriageable and we're having far too much fun to waste our young lives washing other people's socks.'

– 'Because if I had to get into bed with [add name of Smug Married's husband here] just once, let alone every night of the week, I'd tear off my own head and eat it.'

– 'Because actually underneath my clothes my entire body is covered in scales.'

Bad things to say to Smug Marrieds when they ask you why you're not married yet

– (Tearful sheep voice) 'I don't know . . . (sob) Why do you think?'

Good things to say to Radical Feminist Bank Managers

- 'I'm part of a pioneer generation relying on my own economic power, struggling to be freed from centuries of paternalistic sexist oppression. Bastards! Fuckwittage! So can I have a teensy extension on my overdraft, please?'

Bad things to say to Radical Feminist Bank Managers

- 'If you don't lend me enough money to buy outfits, how can I be expected to find anyone rich enough to pay off my overdraft?'

Games

These can be tremendous fun at social occasions when conversation is in danger of drying up, or if guests need distracting from the food. Here is one of my favourites!!

Shag, marry or push off a cliff

In turn, each of the players suggests three names, e.g. Jeffrey Archer, Mohammed Al Fayed, Jonathon Aitken. The person on the player's right must then decide, if they absolutely had to shag one of them, marry another, and push another off a cliff, which it would be.

It is usually best to pick three which are similar in some way.

- Russell Crowe, Mr Darcy, Hugh Grant
- Colonel Gadaffi, the Ayatollah Khomeini, Idi Amin
- Tony Blair, Bill Clinton, Al Gore
- William Hague, Gordon Brown, Robin Cook

It doesn't matter if any of them are dead as it is only a game. This is also tremendous fun with lists of real people whom one knows. (Though this can be a little cruel. And should never be played with lists of people who are actually in the room.)

In Case of Romantic Emergency

Life has its ups, life has its downs! When things go awry in the world of romance, simply follow this easy step-by-step guide.

Emergency First Aid

1 Pour Chardonnay straight down throat.

2 Light cigarette.

3 Put chocolate (or what edible items available) in mouth (cut off any existing mould first so as not to add medical to romantic emergency. Though come to think of it . . . George Clooney . . .)

4 Telephone all nice friends (but not Smug Marrieds or Jellyfishers) and declare State of Emergency.

DO NOT UNDER ANY CIRCUMSTANCES . . .
. . . call him.

It is vital to create a sense of self as aloof now – unavailable ice queen, rather than sheep-voiced sobbing madperson calling obsessively, yelling: 'Bastard. What's wrong with meeeheee?' That way he will quickly start kicking himself.

Good videos to watch till help arrives

Thelma and Louise (Bastards! fuckwittage!)

The Last Seduction (har har that will show them)

Sleepless in Seattle (hope springs eternal)

Pride and Prejudice (wet shirt springs eternal in spite of setbacks)

Gladiator (what one needs is REAL man in skirt)

The Age of Innocence (man prefers older woman)

The Thomas Crown Affair (completely irresistible forty-five-year-old woman love interest)

Titanic – just the bit where the boat splits in half and rears up and everyone slithers down into the freezing sea (better off than them)

Bad videos – not to watch under any circumstances

Fatal Attraction

Great Expectations

(Remember you are not Glenn Close or Miss Havisham but gorgeous newly on-rampage Singleton.)

Bad things to think

- Am too unattractive.

- Am too old.

- Am too fat.

- Am too needy.

- Am too anything.

Good things to think

- Bastards! Fuckwittage!

- Hurrah, am free of evil male oppression!

- Is not me is him, stupid prat.

- Did not want to go out with stupid prat anyway.

- Plenty more non-stupid-prat-style fishes in sea.

- Nothing to do with me: is global epidemic of commitment-phobic men.

- Hurrah, am going to lose weight, get hair cut, develop new positive attitude and totally reinvent self, complete within self as woman of substance.

- I've got all my life to live, and I've got all my love to give and I'll survive, I will survive. I will survive.

The Road to Healing Your Life

With the right tools no problem is insoluble.

Psychiatry

I am not a trained psychiatrist. I do not have certificates and qualifications to hang boastfully on the wall, or a reception area with magazines and a receptionist. And yet I have over twelve years' enviable success as shown in my case histories.

Why Aren't I Good Enough?
– Jude's Story

Jude, an attractive, creative girl in her thirties, was sitting in my consulting room. 'I feel like shit,' she sobbed. 'I'm a fat, useless love pariah. Here, have we run out of Silk Cut?'

'No, I think I've got another pack,' I said, nodding wisely and trying to find my handbag.

'I keep watching all these bloody adverts for deodorants and hatchback cars,' Jude went on, 'and I think I'm supposed to be an anorexic teenage model who runs a top corporation, gets up at 5 a.m., then rushes from the gym to the board meeting and home to wild shagging with perfect husband and children.'

I leaned forward earnestly. 'You think you should shag your own children?'

'Oh for fuck's sake, Bridget. Shag the husband, but

the children and perfect home are in the background. And then I should cook a perfect dinner for twelve people.'

'Uh-huh.' I nodded wisely, taking a large gulp of Chardonnay. 'And how does that make you feel?'

'Like shit, I just bloody well told you,' snarled Jude, lunging at the new packet of Silk Cut. 'If I tried to cook a perfect dinner for twelve people I'd end up in my underwear with wet hair and one foot in a pan of mashed potato shouting: "Oh go fuck yourselves," at the arriving guests.'

The problem seemed insoluble.

Many counsellors do not have the discipline or the tools to really get to the bottom of their patients' problems but I always go to the shop before my consultations and usually think it best to bring at least one extra bottle of Chardonnay just in case. After just a bottle and a half Jude suddenly broke out. 'At last I understand!' she said. 'We are not supposed to be perfect but human beings, and that means being a good friend; being warm, honest, kind, funny and good fun are more important than having a bottom like two billiard balls.'

Thus, as we can see, one does not need a degree in psychiatry to get excellent results!

Miss Havisham Syndrome
– Shazzer's Story

It is a fact of life that psychiatrists must spend huge

amounts of time liberating their patients from ideas and concepts that are clearly outdated. It is indeed tempting for psychiatrists to view themselves as knights of modern science locked in noble combat with the destructive forces of ancient irrational but authoritarian dogma.

Shazzer, an attractive, successful girl in her mid-thirties, with her own job, her own flat and many friends (well, me, Jude and Tom), was sitting in my consulting room. 'I'm Glenn Close from *Fatal Attraction*,' she sobbed, cramming an entire slice of pizza into her mouth so that all the tomato stuff went down her chin. 'I'm Miss Havisham. I'm a tragic pod-womb spinster who goes around thinking the vicar is in love with her.'

'Uh-huh,' I said, nodding wisely and pouring myself another glass of Chardonnay. 'And why do you think that?' I said.

'I just bloody well told you, you paralytic moron,' she said, lighting another Silk Cut from the butt end of her first one. 'I was supposed to go out with this guy Stacey from the gym and he blew me out because he had to work and then I went to the gym and he was sitting doing a salute to the sun in a yoga class. Then I bumped into Magda's Jeremy and told him and he said: "Oh Christ, not another one. We're never going to get you sprogged up at this rate, old girl. Tick-tock, tick-tock."'

'Uh-huh,' I said, nodding wisely and getting another bottle of Chardonnay out of the fridge. 'And what do you think your response to this should be?'

The problem seemed insoluble.

But after just a few more glasses Shazzer had worked it out for herself.

'Bastards! Fuckwittage!' she yelled. 'Spinsters, pah! The whole bloody spinster-on-the-shelf idea is an evil poison hangover from the past, kept alive by an evil paternalistic media. We are a pioneer generation, daring to rely on our own economic power to achieve a good lifestyle instead of marrying bloody men. In years to come there won't be any fuckwit men doing fuckwittage or leaving their wives of thirty years to run off with young bimbos because the women will just laugh in their faces and keep them in kennels as pets! Bastards! Fuckwittage! Singletons, hurrah! 'Ere, pass my that other bol Chardnay willsyoubridge?'

Sexual Sell-By Dates
– Pamela's Story

Pamela Jones, a slightly strange-looking lady in her sixties with large bouffant hair, and a country casuals two-piece in fuchsia with a purple and green leaf motif, was sitting in the Debenhams coffee shop dipping a spoon into a dish of sherry trifle.

'I feel like Germaine bloody Greer and the Invisible Woman,' she burst out. 'All these ridiculous films with Harrison Ford and Clint Eastwood going to bed with women a quarter of their age. You never see it the other way round, do you, Katherine Hepburn with Leonardo DiCaprio? No. No wonder Daddy would rather watch the golf than look at me. Shall we order a coffee ring and a millefeuille?'

'Mmmmm, mmmmm, or maybe a tiramisu,' I murmured, wiping the remains of a chocolate eclair off the plate with my finger. 'Actually, no, I think I'll have a slice of banoffi pie. And how does that make you feel?'

'Absolutely furious, darling,' she said. 'Do you know what? I'm bloody well going to have a vanilla slice as well.'

The problem seemed insoluble.

But then we discovered a whole separate section of different kinds of cheesecake on the menu – raspberry, lemon, blueberry or chocolate fudge swirl with optional creme chantilly piped on the side.

'Actually, it's a load of rubbish,' Mum mumbled brightly as a dribble of raspberry and cream trickled down her chin. 'We're not tubs of cottage cheese on a shelf in Asda. Look at Merle Robertshaw. She married a boy half her age when Wilf died and he's absolutely devoted to her. And he didn't leave much of a fortune didn't Wilf because there isn't a lot of money in meat. And Stanley whatsit from Kettering left Audrey for one of these bimbos – thick as two short planks she was – and after six months he was begging Audrey to take him back and she wouldn't have him. Went off with a boy half her age who owned that little block of shops next to the bypass. Ooh, do you know? I feel slightly ill. Shall we have a creme caramel to settle our stomachs?'

Real Men
– Colin's Story

Colin Jones, an attractive man in his sixties, sporting a yellow diamond-patterned sweater, was sitting in my consulting room. 'I feel like I'm never good enough,' he wailed. 'I only need to leave my socks on the floor for a few days or watch the cricket and rugby all weekend or fart a couple of times and your mother starts rampaging through the house blowing off steam and saying that I think the clitoris is something from Geoffrey Alconbury's lepidoptery collection – ooh, can I have one of those cigarettes? Don't tell your mother.'

'Uh-huh,' I said, nodding wisely and pouring myself another glass of Chardonnay. 'And why do you think she reacts in this way?'

'She doesn't want a real man,' he said, letting out a small belch. 'She's watched too many films and advertisements. She thinks she should have Brad Pitt loading the dishwasher naked and feeding her Haagen-Dazs with a little spoon. Got any more of that whisky, love?'

The problem seemed insoluble.

But once we had been out to the shop for a half bottle of Bells and watched the football for a couple of hours, Dad suddenly broke out. 'She doesn't really want Brad Pitt,' he slurred. 'She likes me because I'm her friend. She once said it's like little kids who have one toy that they like more than all the others and then even when all its fur gets rubbed off they still think it's the most beautiful rabbit in the world. Goal. Gooooooal.'

'Uh-huh,' I said, stumbling slightly as the room seemed to be spinning round and round. 'And when did she say that?'

''Swar two nights ago,' he slurred indistinctly. 'Then I went out to the pub with Geoffrey and when I got back she starts ranting on about it being her birthday or summat. Tell you wor, maybe I should take her out to dinner and buy her a pair of earringssshhh?'

'Blurry good idea,' I said. 'Shwe have anothglass?'

Thus, as we can see, the exercise of psychiatry is a skilled and highly demanding profession. But with the right psychiatric tools no problem is insoluble. Sometimes I think I may start charging for my consultations.

Inner Poise

Self-help books are the new religion.

Spirituality

Self-help books are often ridiculed by others. Of course, they are many and wide-ranging but it can be no coincidence that there was one time in America recently when the top ten bestselling non-fiction books were all self-help books.

I think human beings are like streams, and if one way is blocked to them they find another. Humans need rules for living as nobody has much idea what they are supposed to be doing these days. Therefore, if access to rules disappears with the crumbling of formal religions, humans seek another way to find rules – namely self-help books.

Interestingly, my theory is that many self-help books have basic principles in common with other major world religions, e.g. optimism (see *Emotional Intelligence, You Can Heal Your Life*), confidence in self and general goodness of things (see *Emotional Confidence, How to Get What You Want and Want What You Get*), forgiveness, i.e. not holding on to resentment (see *You Can Heal Your Life, The Seven Habits of Highly Effective People*). These are also found in the Bible ('these three remain: faith, hope and love'). Also staying in the moment is also a common theme (see *You Can Heal Your Life* and Buddhism). Self-help books I would not include in this theory are *How to Rid Your Thighs of Cellulite in 30 Days* (which doesn't work) and *How to Date Women Under Twenty-Five: A Guide for Men Over Forty*.

Other good spiritual notions

Bad things are easier if you are large-spirited and open – e.g. in Buddhism it says a bit of salt in a glass of water is disgusting but if it was a lake you would not even notice it. This helps you not to obsess about things, e.g. say you had a skirt (pink tweedy from Jigsaw) and your friend (Jude) said would you mind if she bought one the same and she would not wear it when you were both out together without asking you. Then she just turned up in it. If you just are relaxed and have lots of things going on you won't really be bothered. But if you're all tight and closed in and small-minded you will start obsessing about it. Maybe for several days. (Bloody Jude. She *said* she would ask me first. And she has loads of clothes.)

Hakuna Matata – this is an African expression much favoured by my mother which means 'don't worry be happy'.

In *Emotional Intelligence* it tells of a woman who had a problem with worrying. She was asked to worry for one minute in a laboratory. She started worrying that she wouldn't be able to worry properly during the minute so that she would be sacked from her treatment for not being worried enough and then her worrying would never be cured so her life would be ruined. Which I thought showed how stupid worrying is, if you can possibly avoid it.

(Bloody Jude. She definitely said she would ask me before wearing the skirt. I would not mind if she did not have many clothes but she does. Humph.)

Basic spiritual principles

These then are the basic spiritual principles for developing inner poise:

- Not worrying but instead thinking everything will be all right as it probably will.

- Living in the moment and not regretting things or fantasizing (esp. re: fuckwits).

- Not getting obsessed by things.

- Not getting a hate-on with people but just forgetting about it and thinking about something else if they annoy you.

Mantras

Often at trying times it is good to repeat mantras, e.g.:

- Am assured, receptive, responsive woman of substance. My sense of self comes from the outside world and not within.

- Inner poise, inner poise.

- Am not a glass of water but a Buddhist lake.
  Am not a glass of water but a Buddhist lake.

(Sometimes it is better not to say them out loud.)

(Bloody Jude.)

How to Lose Weight

The important thing is that diets are not made to be picked and mixed but stuck to – which is exactly what I intend to do once I've eaten this chocolate croissant.

Weight-Loss Tips

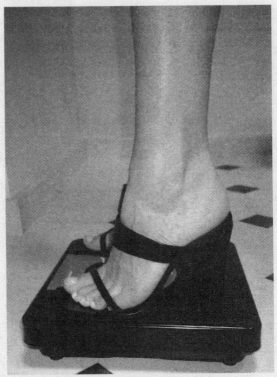

Always wear 3-inch heels when weighing . . .

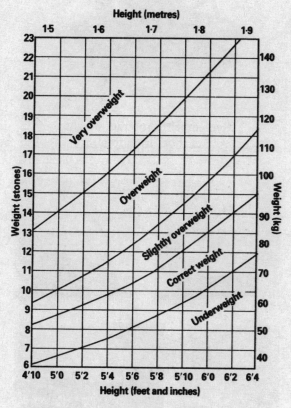

Height (metres)

Very overweight

Overweight

Slightly overweight

Correct weight

Underweight

Weight (stones)

Weight (kg)

Height (feet and inches)

. . . to create impressive weight to height ratio.

Remember to subtract weight
of shoes from total.

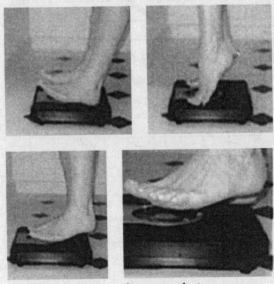

Then experiment with your scales' responses . . .

. . . simple hand pressure can reduce weight
by several pounds. There.

Feng Shui

This is all to do with mapping the ba-gua of your flat and putting things in pairs everywhere to create a karma of being in a couple.

The only really important thing is not to put a waste-paper basket in your Relationship Corner.

Useful Terms and Words
for Practical Living

Aargh aargh.

Answerphone substitute for normal human partner.

Bunny boiler hateful poison concept suggesting that if a woman is thirty-six and unmarried she is going to start murdering other people's husbands and boiling their children's rabbits.

Commitment phobic person who insists on describing anything from shag to fourteen-year relationship as 'just good friends'.

Communal changing room hateful place always containing the girl who looks fantastic in everything and swings around smirking at your thighs, flicking her hair and doing model poses in the mirror saying: 'Does it make me look fat?' to her obligatory obese friend who looks like a water buffalo in everything.

Daniel fuckwit that I used to go out with.

Emotional Fuckwittage annoying behaviour by fuckwits, e.g. saying will ring then not ringing, shagging others then not calling them, being in relationships with others then saying it's not a relationship, going out with people for twelve years whilst insisting they don't want to get too serious, refusing to go on mini-breaks, etc. etc.

Fuckwit person (man) who does emotional fuckwitt-age.

Fuckwittage (the French pronunciation) verb: fuck-witted behaviour.

g. good.

Gaaah! expression of shock on discovering self forty-five minutes late for work, or love interest forty-five minutes early for date.

Hag fag gay male friend ideal for thirty-something female Singleton, since understands what is like to be treated as disappointment to parents and freak by society. Also excellent for outfit choice assistance.

Humph useful expression for showing disgruntlement.

I rarely used word normally replaced by 'self'.

Jellyfisher person who drops little verbal stings into conversation which you hardly notice at time but leave you feeling hurt afterwards whilst not pinpoint-ing exactly where came from, e.g. 'Just seen some great trousers, well, unless you have cellulite jodhpurs, of course.' (Portuguese Man of War variety)

Jude lovely Singleton friend with whizzy job in the City: better at dealing with collapse of the Yen than commitment-phobic non-boyfriend Vile Richard.

Karma v. important but incomprehensible concept.

Lettuce rare foodstuff which uses up more calories to chew than it contains.

Mentionitis when someone's name keeps coming up when not strictly relevant, e.g. 'Rebecca has a car like that', or 'Rebecca likes fish', thereby suggesting said person performing Mentionitis has crush on said Rebecca. Especially if one is paranoid.

Mini-break important rite-of-relationship-passage involving stay of not less than one and not more than three nights in country house/hotel/fisherman's cottage, near pub by river (ideally with open fire) in country, e.g. Cornwall or similar. Mini-breaks clearly demonstrate that a man has sufficient romantic interest in you to come away from football and thus that you are having a relationship and not just shagging.

Natural look only achieved for date after several hours of farming techniques – harvesting, crop-spraying, filing, waxing, plucking, exfoliating, etc. Never actually let yourself revert to nature or you will end up with a full beard and handlebar moustache on each shin.

One-Four-Seven-One telephonic device which adds to excitement of being single but also doubles misery potential on arrival home: no-number stored-on-1471 misery adds to no-message-on-answerphone misery, or number-stored-turning-out-to-be-mother's misery.

Pashmina pretentious scarf thing but, more importantly, pashmina is platonic friend who makes you feel small because you know you want to shag him more than he wants to shag you.

Pashmarried platonic friend whom you used to go out with and is now married with children, likes having you around as memory of old life, but makes you feel like mad barren pod-womb imagining vicar is in love with self.

Pashmincer platonic friend who you fancy but unfortunately is gay.

Pashspurt 'platonic friend' who keeps making passes then getting cross when you say you just want to be friends.

Quince fruit-type thing beginning with 'q' unlike any other words can think of.

Re-tread hideous poison concept generated by misguided journalist that thirty-something girls are the sort of girls you wanted to go out with when they were in their twenties and they wouldn't and now you can go out with them but don't want to. Said misguided journalist now happily ensconced with thirty-something girl plus baby thereby proving whole concept was load of old bollocks.

Self-control alien concept, not necessarily desirable –
look at Pol Pot.

Shazzer lovely Singleton friend: top radical feminist
except when sobbing in sheep's voice over boys she
met in gym.

Singleton replacement for poison outdated word
'spinster'.

Smug Married annoying married person who says
things like 'Why aren't you married yet?' 'How's your
love life' and 'Can't put it off for ever, you know, tick-
tock, tick-tock.'

Tom best gay friend who always greets self with
'Bridget, you've lost so much weight.' Which is nice.

Urban family select group of Singleton friends who
perform function of old-fashioned blood family only
do all communication over phone or e-mail unless in-
volves Chardonnay.

Valentine's Day purely cynical commercial enter-
prise unless you get one and then it's a marvellous
vehicle for people to show their appreciation of others
who more than deserve it: rather like awards at award
ceremonies.

v.g. very good.

Why frequently asked question, e.g. Why do Smug
Marrieds/fuckwits do this? Why?

X person who should never go off with anyone else but remain celibate to the end of their days in order to provide you with a mental fallback position.

Zen something which, when you look at life, can be applied to anything: Zen and the art of shopping, Zen and the art of blow-drying, Zen and the art of vat returns, etc. etc. It is all a question of flow rather than struggle. But Jude says not to mention this to Shazzer as she thinks it is bollocks.

The Comic Relief Guide to Changing a Life

£2 from every copy of *Bridget Jones's Guide to Life* will go to Comic Relief.

Every penny of that £2 will help poor and disadvantaged people in Africa and the UK to help themselves – it's about giving them a leg-up, not a handout.

Since Comic Relief was set up in 1985, it's raised an amazing £174m, and with your help there's more to come. Here's how some of the cash is making a difference.

- **25p** in the UK covers the cost of calling a refuge to find a safe place to stay for a woman and her children fleeing domestic violence.

- **25p** will cover the cost of a phone call a vulnerable older person makes to a helpline – it could be their lifeline.

- **30p** will pay for a bag of seeds for a farmer in Ethiopia to plant trees to help make his land less vulnerable to the effects of flooding.

- **35p** will buy 7 sachets of oral rehydration salts to help save a child in Africa from dying of diarrhoea.

- **£1** pays for one day's tailoring training for an orphan in Rwanda to help learn a trade to earn a living.

If you'd like to know more about Comic Relief, log on to www.comicrelief.com, or write to:
Comic Relief, 5th Floor, 89 Albert Embankment, London SE1 7TP.
Registered Charity Number 326568.